LADY BIRD, QUICKLY

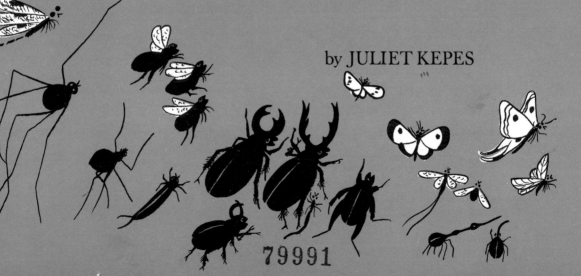

QUICKLY

by JULIET KEPES

An Atlantic Monthly Press Book   Little, Brown and Company   BOSTON · TORONTO

To Rasheed
if he will
only sit still
long enough
to read it

Second Printing

Atlantic—Little, Brown books are published
by Little, Brown and Company in association
with the Atlantic Monthly Press
*Published simultaneously in Canada
by Little, Brown & Company (Canada) Limited*
PRINTED IN THE UNITED STATES OF AMERICA

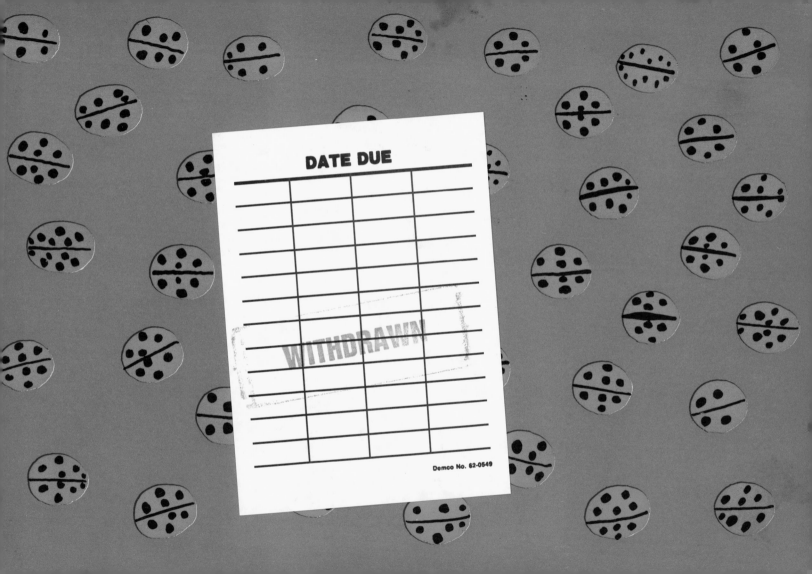

LADY BIRD, QUICKLY

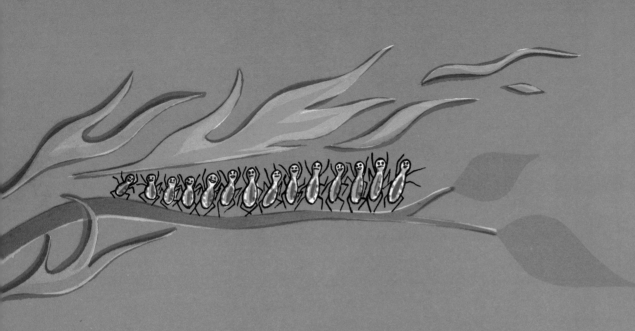

"Lady Bird, Lady Bird, fly away home,   Your house is on fire,
                                                    your children alone."

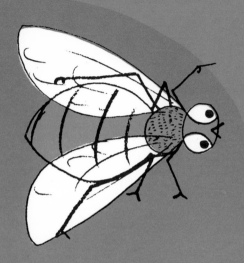

The fly told the wasp.

And the wasp told the spider,   "Lady Bird, Lady Bird, fly away home."

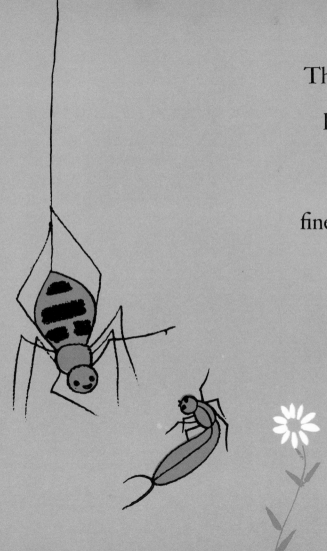

The spider

let down

a very

fine thread.

And he told the earwig.

Earwig scampered to tell

the green grasshoppers,

"Lady Bird, Lady Bird, fly away home."

The grasshoppers whirred it into a tune.

"Lady Bird, Lady Bird, fly away home."

13

Cicada joined in,   chirruping loudly to all the black ants,

"Lady Bird, Lady Bird, fly away home."

to three sturdy stag beetles,

The ants passed the message

17

who told daddy-longlegs,

who told the gay dragonflies,

"Lady Bird, Lady Bird,

fly away home."

Swooping and gliding above the blue pond

the dragonflies called down to a water bug paddling,

"Lady Bird,

Lady Bird,

fly away home."

Busy water bug told a bee passing by.

buzzing

and

Humming

bee

flew to the flowers.

"Lady Bird, Lady Bird, fly   away home."

25

The buzzing was carried

from blossom

to blossom,

to bright-colored butterfly,

Mayfly and gadfly.

"Lady Bird, Lady Bird, fly away home."

Their voices were hurried along on the breeze

to stick insect

and weevil.

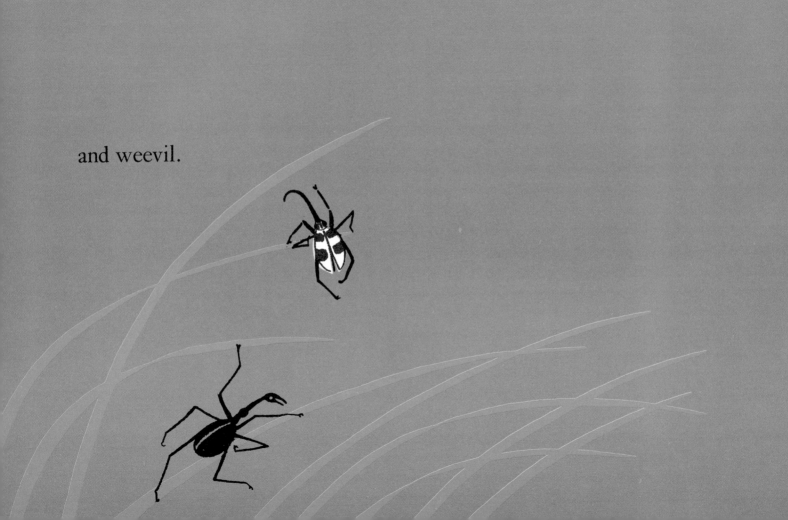

"Lady Bird, Lady Bird, fly away home."

Fluttering moths heard the echo at dusk,

"Lady Bird, Lady Bird, fly away home."

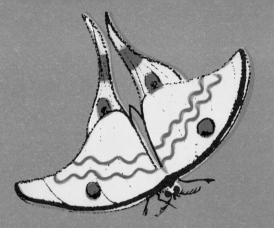

Moths saw the lady bird flitting nearby.

They stopped her to tell her before she went further,

"Your house is on fire, your children alone."

Lady bird quickly flew fast as she could

to her tree on the hilltop.

It was flashing and sparkling,

aflicker with fire, like candles at Christmas.

There were her children

quite safe, not alone,

with thousands of fireflies,

each bobbing a light.

Dancing and prancing,

and singing the song

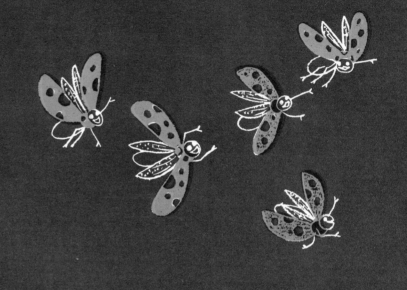

"Lady Bird, Lady Bird, fly away home."

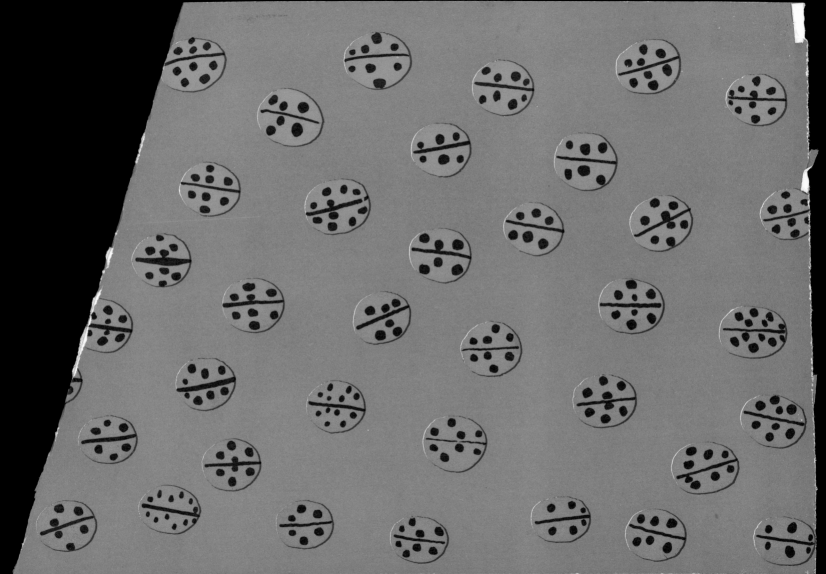

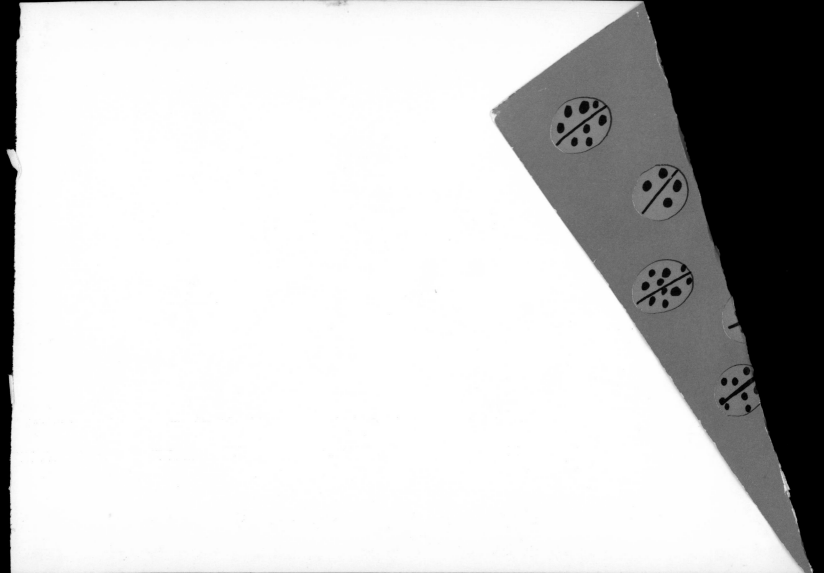